Funny Sort of Treasure

Roderick Hunt

Illustrated by Alex Brychta

OXFORD
UNIVERSITY PRESS

OXFORD

UNIVERSITY PRESS

Great Clarendon Street, Oxford, OX2 6DP

Oxford   New York
Athens   Auckland   Bangkok   Bogotá   Buenos Aires   Calcutta
Cape Town   Chennai   Dar es Salaam   Delhi   Florence   Hong Kong
Istanbul   Karachi   Kuala Lumpur   Madrid   Melbourne   Mexico City
Mumbai   Nairobi   Paris   São Paulo   Singapore   Taipei   Tokyo
Toronto   Warsaw

and associated companies in
Berlin   Ibadan

Oxford is a trade mark of Oxford University Press

© text Roderick Hunt 1998
© illustrations Alex Brychta
First Published 1998
Reprinted 1999

ISBN 019 918663 4

Printed in Hong Kong

Chapter 1

Andy had a roll of paper with a red ribbon round it.

'Look at this, Chris,' he said. He unrolled the paper.

It was a treasure map. Chris looked at it and gasped. 'It's amazing,' he said.

The map had drawings on it. There was a cross by a tree. It said, 'Dig here.'

'It looks really good,' said Chris. 'How long did you take to draw it?'

'All weekend,' said Andy.

'Miss Teal will like it,' said Chris. 'I bet she puts it on the wall.'

Chris had drawn a map, too. 'It's not as good as yours,' he told Andy.

Miss Teal's class was doing a project on maps. Everyone was enjoying it.

No one thought the map project would lead to trouble.

Chapter 2

That evening, Miss Teal went to
Wolf Hill School. She took her
boyfriend with her. 'I want you to
help,' she said.

They went on to the school field.
Miss Teal had lots of little pegs. The
pegs had bits of red wool on them.

'They're for my lesson about maps,' she said.

Miss Teal pushed a few pegs into the ground. 'Can you see them, John?' she said. 'Can you see the wool?'

John sighed. 'Yes,' he said. 'But you have to look hard. The grass is long.'

'Right,' said Miss Teal. 'I've got a hundred pegs. Put them in little groups all over the field.'

'What a way to spend the evening!' said John. 'I hope it's an interesting lesson.'

It was an interesting lesson – but it didn't go quite as Miss Teal had planned.

Chapter 3

In the morning, Chris called for
Andy. They started out for school.
On the way they met Kat and Gizmo.
Kat had a bag. A long tube stuck out
of it.

'What's in the tube?' asked Chris.

'It's my treasure map,' said Kat. 'It's quite big. I didn't want to fold it.'

'Wait until you see Andy's map,' said Chris. 'It's amazing.'

Andy stopped. He hit his head with the palm of his hand.

'Oh no!' he groaned. 'I've left my treasure map at home.'

'Never mind,' said Kat. 'We'll go back home with you. If we run we won't be late.'

They were nearly late. Gizmo got a bit wheezy. He couldn't run. By the time they got to school, the bell was ringing.

Chapter 4

All the children had treasure maps. Miss Teal looked at them. 'Well done,' she said. 'The maps are wonderful.'

Most of the maps were of made-up places. Some of them were of islands. Kat's map looked old and brown. 'My mum put it in the oven,' she said.

Andy's map was different. It had little drawings on it. Miss Teal looked at the map closely. 'The drawings are amazing, Andy,' she said.

It was a map of the school. It showed the roads around it. It showed the playground and the field. The treasure cross was on the field.

'I wish there really was treasure on the field,' said Andy.

Miss Teal laughed. 'Well, we can't dig the field up to see,' she said.

In the end there was treasure on the field. It was not the kind of treasure anyone expected.

Chapter 5

Miss Teal had a surprise for her class. She took them on to the field.

'This is part of the map project,' she said. 'I want you to work in groups of six.'

Loz looked at the ground. 'I can see bits of wool everywhere,' she said.

'They're on little pegs,' said Najma.

'I know,' said Miss Teal. 'I put them there. They're for our map project.'

Miss Teal gave each group some string. 'Use the string to make a large square,' she said.

'Why?' asked Michael Ward.

'There will be pegs in your square. I want you to make a map of them. How could you do that?'

'I know,' said Kat. 'We can make a grid.'

Just then, a tractor drove on to the field. It was Mr Minns with his gang mower. He had come to cut the grass.

Chapter 6

Mr Minns stopped the tractor. He began to set the blades of the mower. Miss Teal gasped. She ran over to Mr Minns.

'Stop!' called Miss Teal. 'You can't cut the grass now. I'm using the field for a lesson. I've put wool all over it!'

Mr Minns shook his head.

Miss Teal told him about her lesson.
'I want the children to mark out
grids,' she said.

'Yes,' said Kat. 'We're going to
make maps.'

Mr Minns sniffed. 'I can't help that,' he said. 'I'm booked to cut the grass. I can't hang about while you look for bits of wool.'

Everyone was upset.

'Does this mean we can't do the lesson?' said Michael Ward.

Mr Minns sniffed again. He didn't want to upset Miss Teal. 'I'm sorry,' he said. 'I have to cut three fields today. I must cut this one now.'

'Please, Miss Teal, shall I get Mr Saffrey?' asked Chris.

Chapter 7

Mr Saffrey came quickly. Miss Teal told him about her lesson. She told him about all the little pegs.

Mr Minns told Mr Saffrey how busy he was. 'Grass won't wait,' he said. 'It has to be cut.'

Mr Saffrey rubbed his beard. 'Oh
dear,' he said. He thought hard.
Then he spoke to Mr Minns.

'Miss Teal does need the field. Will
you wait for an hour? We will pay
you extra.'

Mr Minns thought for a bit. 'All
right,' he said. 'I'll have my coffee
now.'

Mr Saffrey smiled at the children. 'You can use the field after all,' he said.

He looked at Miss Teal. 'I'm going to the bank,' he said. 'I won't be long.'

Mr Saffrey ran into trouble at the bank. He was back sooner than anyone expected.

Chapter 8

Mr Saffrey drove to the bank. He went in the school mini-bus. There was nowhere to park. 'I'll wait for a space,' he thought.

A security truck was outside the bank. Two guards were unloading bags full of money.

Suddenly, a car skidded and stopped. Two people jumped out. They wore masks. One of them shouted 'Freeze!'

'Oh no!' thought Mr Saffrey. 'It's a hold up!'

The robbers grabbed the bags of money. They jumped in the car and raced away.

Mr Saffrey didn't stop to think. He drove the mini-bus in front of the car. The car skidded. It hit the side of the mini-bus. There was a loud crash.

'Oh no!' thought Mr Saffrey. 'What have I done?'

Chapter 9

The robbers tried to start the car. It wouldn't go. Steam hissed from the front of it. The horn was going.

One of them jumped out of the car. Mr Saffrey gasped. The robber was a woman. She had one of the money bags in her hand.

The robber ran down the street.
She ran towards Wolf Hill School.

'Stop!' shouted Mr Saffrey.

He drove after her in the mini-bus.
The mini-bus made a funny clanking
noise.

The robber reached the school fence. Mr Saffrey was catching up with her. Suddenly there was a bang. The mini-bus stopped. Smoke poured out of it.

The robber jumped over the fence. She began to run across the field.

Mr Minns was sitting on his tractor. He was drinking his coffee. The robber ran past him.

'Stop, thief!' shouted Mr Saffrey.

Chapter 10

Andy and Chris had worked with Gizmo, Kat, Loz and Najma. Miss Teal called the class together. 'I want to see all the grids,' she said.

They heard a shout. 'Stop, thief!'

It was Mr Saffrey. Then they heard Mr Minns start his tractor.

Gizmo pointed. His mouth fell open. 'Look!' he gasped.

The robber was running across the field. She was holding a big bag. Something was falling out of it.

Mr Minns revved up the tractor.
He began to chase the robber.

The tractor picked up speed. It was
towing the gang mower. Grass flew
up from the blades like a green
fountain.

The robber ran faster. Money was dropping out of the bag. One or two notes fell out . . . then ten . . . then twenty . . . then hundreds.

The robber hadn't noticed. Neither had Mr Minns.

Chapter 11

The gang mower sliced over the money. There was a chopping noise. The notes were sliced in half. Some were sliced in pieces. The bits of money flew up in the air. Grass and paper fell back on to the field.

The robber ran into one of the
children's grids. Her feet caught in
the string. She fell over with a thud.

Mr Minns stopped his tractor. Mr
Saffrey ran across the field. 'Got
you!' said Mr Minns.

The robber looked at the empty bag. All of the money was gone. The children looked at the field. There was paper everywhere.

They walked across the grass. No one said a word.

They started picking up bits of bank notes.

Chapter 12

There was money everywhere.

Loz, Chris and Najma went to their grid.

'Wow!' said Chris. 'These were fifty-pound notes, once.'

Najma looked at the grid. 'There's a lot of money here,' she said. 'There must be hundreds of pounds.'

'It's like finding treasure,' said Gizmo. 'It's just as if your treasure map has come true.'

'We can't keep it,' said Andy.

Chris had an idea. He took off his sweater and held it like a bag. 'Put all the bits in here,' he said.

They heard Mr Saffrey shouting. He had a large box. 'I want every single bit in this box,' he said. 'Don't you dare try and keep any!'

Chapter 13

It was assembly time. Everyone was in the hall. Mr Saffrey locked his bony fingers together. Then he made them click.

'I wish he wouldn't do that,' said Najma.

Mr Saffrey had someone with him. She was the manager of the bank.

'Miss Teal's class did well,' said Mr Saffrey. 'They picked up all of the money before it blew away. None of it was missing. Who can guess how much money there was?'

Chris put up his hand. 'A thousand pounds?' he guessed.

The bank manager smiled. 'I can tell you,' she said. 'There was fifty thousand pounds.'

Everyone gasped.

'There will be a reward for the school,' she said.

Mr Saffrey thought of the school mini-bus. It had been bashed in by the robbers' car.

'Perhaps we can repair the mini-bus,' he said.

Chapter 14

That was how Wolf Hill School got a brand new mini-bus.

The bank gave it to them as a reward.

Miss Teal's class had their picture in the paper.

'Andy's treasure map came true, in a way,' said Chris 'We did find a funny sort of treasure.'